HOPSCOTCH

I Can't Stand It!

First published in 2004 by
Franklin Watts
96 Leonard Street
London
EC2A 4XD

Franklin Watts Australia
45–51 Huntley Street
Alexandria
NSW 2015

A CIP catalogue record for this book is available
from the British Library.

ISBN 0 7496 5727 8 (hbk)
ISBN 0 7496 5765 0 (pbk)

Series Editor: Jackie Hamley
Series Advisor: Dr Barrie Wade
Cover Design: Jason Anscomb
Design: Peter Scoulding

Printed in Hong Kong / China

I Can't
Stand It!

by Anne Adeney and Mike Phillips

W
FRANKLIN WATTS
LONDON·SYDNEY

Sam's house was very small.

Sam's house was very noisy.

The tap dripped: *drip-drop*.

His wife's knitting needles clicked:
click-clack.

The door squeaked back and forth
in the breeze: *squeeeak.*

SQUEEEAK!

Sam put his hands over his ears,
but he could still hear everything.

DRIP-DROP!   CLICK-CLACK!

SQEEEEEAK!

The grandfather clock ticked: *tick-tock.*

TICK-TOCK!

The floorboards creaked as the cat walked on them: *purr-purr, creeeak.*

PURR! PURR!

CREEEAK!

Drip-drop, click-clack, squeeeak,

tick-tock, purr-purr, creeeak!

"I can't stand this noise any

longer!" said Sam.

He ran out of the house and went
to see the Wise Woman.

"Help me!" begged Sam.
"My house is too small and
too noisy. I can't stand it!"

The Wise Woman looked wise and thought about the problem.

Then she said something amazing:
"Put all your animals into the
house."

Sam ran home as fast as he could.

All the way home he thought:

"*Put all your animals into the house.*

How silly is that!"

TICK-TOCK! PURR! CLICK-CLACK! SQUEEEAK! PURR! CREEEAK! DRIP-DROP!

Sam sat down again and heard:

Drip-drop, click-clack, squeeeak,

tick-tock, purr-purr, creeeak!

"I can't stand this noise!" he cried.

Sam went out into the
farmyard and brought all
his animals into the house.
The animals filled the
house to bursting.

His wife had a chicken on her head
and another one on her knitting
needles: *cluck-cluck.*

The cows were helping themselves
to dinner from the table: *moo-moo.*

The sheep were everywhere.

Some were sitting in Sam's chair

by the fire: *baa-baa*.

The cat was being squeezed out of her basket by some piglets: *oink-oink*.

The horse was eating Sam's wife's straw hat: *neigh-neigh*.

Cluck-cluck, moo-moo, baa,

oink-oink, neigh-neigh, baa!

"This is terrible!" shouted Sam.

"I can't STAND it!"

Sam crawled under the horse ...

... climbed over the cow ...

... and pushed his way through
the flock of sheep.

23

Sam ran back to the Wise Woman's house. "My house is VERY small and VERY noisy!" he wailed.

The Wise Woman looked wise and
thought about the problem.
Then she said something amazing:
"Take all your animals out of
the house."

Sam ran home as fast as he could. He herded the animals back to the barn and stables.

Then Sam went into his house. Now he could stretch his arms in every direction. What a *big* house he had!

He sat down in his chair. He couldn't hear all the animals. What a *quiet* house he had!

"That's *much* better!" said Sam,

"a big, quiet house!"

Hopscotch has been specially designed to fit the requirements of the National Literacy Strategy. It offers real books by top authors and illustrators for children developing their reading skills.

There are 21 Hopscotch stories to choose from:

Marvin, the Blue Pig
Written by Karen Wallace
Illustrated by Lisa Williams

Plip and Plop
Written by Penny Dolan
Illustrated by Lisa Smith

The Queen's Dragon
Written by Anne Cassidy
Illustrated by Gwyneth Williamson

Flora McQuack
Written by Penny Dolan
Illustrated by Kay Widdowson

Willie the Whale
Written by Joy Oades
Illustrated by Barbara Vagnozzi

Naughty Nancy
Written by Anne Cassidy
Illustrated by Desideria Guicciardini

Run!
Written by Sue Ferraby
Illustrated by Fabiano Fiorin

The Playground Snake
Written by Brian Moses
Illustrated by David Mostyn

"Sausages!"
Written by Anne Adeney
Illustrated by Roger Fereday

The Truth about Hansel and Gretel
Written by Karina Law
Illustrated by Elke Counsell

Pippin's Big Jump
Written by Hilary Robinson
Illustrated by Sarah Warburton

Whose Birthday Is It?
Written by Sherryl Clark
Illustrated by Jan Smith

The Princess and the Frog
Written by Margaret Nash
Illustrated by Martin Remphry

Flynn Flies High
Written by Hilary Robinson
Illustrated by Tim Archbold

Clever Cat
Written by Karen Wallace
Illustrated by Anni Axworthy

Moo!
Written by Penny Dolan
Illustrated by Melanie Sharp

Izzie's Idea
Written by Jillian Powell
Illustrated by Leonie Shearing

Roly-poly Rice Ball
Written by Penny Dolan
Illustrated by Diana Mayo

I Can't Stand It!
Written by Anne Adeney
Illustrated by Mike Phillips

Cockerel's Big Egg
Written by Damian Harvey
Illustrated by François Hall

The Truth about those Billy Goats
Written by Karina Law
Illustrated by Graham Philpot

by Laura North and Scoular Anderson

W

150431357

This story is based on
The Pied Piper of Hamel...
You can read the origin...
Hopscotch Fairy Tales. Can you...
up your own twist for the story?

First published in 2013 by
Franklin Watts
338 Euston Road
London
NW1 3BH

Franklin Watts Australia
Level 17/207 Kent Street
Sydney
NSW 2000

A CIP catalogue record for this book is available
from the British Library.

ISBN 978 1 4451 1632 7 (hbk)
ISBN 978 1 4451 1638 9 (pbk)

Series Editor: Melanie Palmer
Series Advisor: Catherine Glavina
Series Designer: Peter Scoulding

Printed in China

Franklin Watts is a division of
Hachette Children's Books,
an Hachette UK company
www.hachette.co.uk

To Dylan — L.N.